The Portrait of a Lady

HENRY JAMES

Level 3

Retold by Janet McAlpin
Series Editors: andy Hopkins and Jocelyn Potter

Pearson Education Limited
Edinburgh Gate, Harlow,
Essex CM20 2JE, England
and Associated Companies throughout the world.

ISBN 0 582 41783 X

First published 1881
This adaptation first published by Penguin Books 1997
Published by Addison Wesley Longman Limited
and Penguin Books Ltd. 1998
New edition first published 1999

Second impression 2000

Text copyright © Janet McAlpin 1997
Illustrations copyright © Victor Ambrus 1997
All rights reserved

The moral right of the adapter and of the illustrator has been asserted

Set in 11/14pt Monotype Bembo by
Rowland Phototypesetting Ltd,
Bury St Edmunds, Suffolk
Printed in Spain by Mateu Cromo, S.A. Pinto (Madrid)

Published by Pearson Education Limited in association with
Penguin Books Ltd., both companies being subsidiaries of Pearson Plc

For a complete list of the titles available in the Penguin Readers series please write to your
local Pearson Education office or to: Marketing Department, Penguin Longman Publishing,
5 Bentinck Street, London W1M 5RN.

Contents

Introduction

'I thank you more than I can say, my lord, but I am not sure I want to marry anyone.'

This is how Isabel Archer answers Lord Warburton when he first asks her to marry him. Isabel is an intelligent young American woman whose father has just died. Her aunt, Mrs Touchett, invites her to visit Europe. In England she meets her rich uncle and her cousin Ralph. Two other rich men, Caspar Goodwood and Lord Warburton, would like to marry her but Isabel wants to travel, to meet new people and to learn about the world. She and her cousin Ralph become good friends. When Ralph's father dies, Isabel is surprised to learn that he has left her a lot of money: seventy thousand pounds.

When staying in Italy with her aunt, Isabel meets an American art lover, Gilbert Osmond. He is not rich, so she agrees to marry him, believing that her money can help him. Too late, she realizes that she has made a bad mistake. Osmond only cares about her money and doesn't really love her. He tries to get his daughter Pansy to marry Lord Warburton because he is rich and famous, knowing that Pansy is already happily in love with a younger man. When Isabel realizes Osmond's plan, she says that she will not help him and this makes Osmond very angry. By the end of the story Isabel understands who her real friends are. She is a sadder but wiser young lady.

Henry James was an American, born in New York in 1843. His father was a well-known writer and his brother, William James, was a famous university teacher. As a young man, James spent a lot of time travelling in Europe and he also studied law at Harvard University. He wrote his first stories in 1865. He moved to England in 1876 and decided to stay there but he also continued to make visits to France and Italy.

He lived in the small town of Rye on the south coast and became friends with many famous writers, among them Joseph Conrad, Ford Madox Ford and H. G. Wells. In 1915, James decided to become British. The King of England gave him the Order of Merit (a title which the king or queen gives to people who are successful in different areas of national life). James died the following year.

Henry James wrote many famous books, among them *Washington Square* (1880), *The Bostonians* (1886), *What Maisie Knew* (1887), *The Wings of a Dove* (1902), *The Ambassadors* (1903), and *The Golden Bowl* (1904). He started to write *The Portrait of a Lady* in 1880, when he was staying for some months in Florence. The book was immediately successful, both in Britain and the United States.

Henry James was interested in the way that people think and feel. The people he wrote about were usually people with plenty of money, who liked to travel around the world. He liked to describe young Americans visiting Europe and making friends with Europeans. The Americans in his stories are usually open-hearted and the Europeans are often clever, selfish and mainly interested in money. In this story, the dishonest people, Gilbert Osmond and Madame Merle, are in fact Americans but Americans who have liked in Europe for many years. The fortune which Ralph asks his father to give Isabel does not make her freer. In fact, it is the reason why Gilbert Osmond wants to marry her. He is not interested in her as a person: 'She has too many ideas.' Isabel wants to use her money to help other people and this is mainly why she agrees to marry Osmond.

Love, marriage, friendship and money are the things that lie at the heart of this story. With these important subjects, it is not surprising that *The Portrait of a Lady* is one of Henry James's best-loved books.

Chapter 1   Isabel's Two Visitors

One wet spring afternoon Isabel Archer had two visitors. The first was an old lady in a big raincoat. Isabel did not know her. She put down the book that she was reading and stood up.

'I guess you're one of my sister's daughters,' said the stranger.

'Ah,' said Isabel slowly, 'then I guess you're our bad Aunt Lydia.'

'Yes, I am your aunt,' said the woman, 'but I'm not bad. Did your father say that? He didn't like me. We never spoke again after your mother died. Which daughter are you?'

'I'm Isabel, the youngest,' said Isabel.

'And are you the prettiest?'

'I have no idea,' said Isabel.

'I'm sure you are.'

And in that way, Isabel and her aunt made friends.

They talked for an hour, about Isabel's two married sisters, about their father, and about the house. Isabel and her sisters were selling the house.

'We can't keep it,' explained Isabel, 'because father didn't leave much money when he died. But I'm sorry. This was my grandmother's house, and I love it.'

'I don't see why,' said her aunt. 'Your father died here.'

'A great many people have died here,' said Isabel, 'and a great many people have lived here. This old house is full of past times. That's why I like it.'

'If you like the past you must leave America,' said her aunt. 'Come to Italy. That's where I live. My house in Florence is very, very old.'

'Florence?' said Isabel. 'Don't you live in England?'

'My husband lives in England and I live in Florence,' said Isabel's aunt. 'You shall see both. Leave it to me.'

When her aunt returned to her hotel, Isabel tried to return to her book, but her thoughts were everywhere. She was very happy in America, but she also wanted to see Europe. She was more serious and intelligent than her sisters, and she wanted to learn as much as possible.

Some time later, her second visitor arrived. This time, Isabel was not surprised. Caspar Goodwood lived in Boston, but his business often brought him to New York. He always wrote a letter before he came. He thought Isabel was the most beautiful young woman of her time.

And Caspar Goodwood was the finest young man that Isabel knew. He was tall and strong, like a soldier, perhaps a little too square, but handsome and brown. When he came into the room his blue eyes were full of hope. Isabel could see that he wanted to speak of marriage, but after half an hour she sent him away. When he left, he was not smiling.

Chapter 2   Tea in an English Garden

In summer, Mr Touchett liked to take afternoon tea in his garden. He drank it very slowly. His cup was big, with bright colours, and very old – much older than Mr Touchett. Not far away, his son Ralph walked with Lord Warburton. They were smoking cigarettes. Two dogs watched the men.

Ralph Touchett loved his father. They were American, but Ralph was a small boy when his father came to live in England. At that time Mr Touchett worked for an American bank. He was an old man now – old, and sick, and very rich, but he didn't want to return to America. He loved his old English house with its great garden.

His wife did not love England. Did she love Mr Touchett? It was difficult to say. She certainly loved her son Ralph, and they spent three months of every year together. Ralph was sick too. In the summer he stayed in England with his father. In the winter he visited his mother in Florence. Ralph needed the sun.

Ralph was speaking to Lord Warburton about his cousin. 'Her name is Isabel,' he said. 'My mother has just arrived with her from America. Look, here she comes.'

Isabel came out of the house and Ralph went to meet her. The smaller dog ran up to her. She picked it up and smiled. 'Is this your little dog?' she asked Ralph.

'He was,' said Ralph, 'but I think he loves you now.'

Isabel smiled again. 'Your mother is in her room,' she said. 'Can you please go to her at seven o'clock?'

'Of course,' said Ralph. 'Now please come and meet my father and our neighbour, Lord Warburton.'

'My dear,' said Mr Touchett, 'you must have some tea. Where is my wife?'

'She is in her room, Daddy,' said Ralph.

'Then perhaps I'll see her at dinner,' said his father.

Isabel sat down with the little dog. Her dress was black because her father was dead, but her eyes were bright and quick. 'How perfect it is here,' she said, 'the river, the garden, your beautiful old house . . .'

'Miss Archer,' said Lord Warburton, 'if you like old places you must visit my house.'

Isabel asked about his family. Lord Warburton had two younger brothers and four sisters. Both his parents were dead. One brother was a soldier and the other was in the church. 'They're all good people,' he explained. 'Not specially clever, but pleasant and good.' Isabel agreed to meet his sisters.

A man brought Lord Warburton's horse and Ralph went to

3

'You once wanted to know my idea of an interesting woman,'
Lord Warburton said to Ralph. 'Well there it is.'

say goodbye. Lord Warburton looked back at Isabel. 'You once wanted to know my idea of an interesting woman,' Lord Warburton said to Ralph. 'Well, there it is.'

Chapter 3   Mrs Touchett's Plans for Isabel

At seven o'clock Ralph went to his mother's room. She was dressed for dinner. She kissed him and asked about her husband's health. Then she asked about Ralph's health. The news was not very good about either of them.

'It's the English weather,' said Mrs Touchett. 'That's why I live in Florence.'

Ralph smiled. 'I'll come to Italy in the winter, dear mother,' he said. 'Now tell me about the young lady. What will you do with her?'

'I want her to stay here for a month. Then I will take her to Paris. She needs clothes to wear in Florence.'

'Of course,' said Ralph. 'But I mean, what will you do with her in a more general way?'

'I will show her four European countries and she will learn perfect French. She already knows it very well.'

Ralph said, 'That sounds very dry.'

Mrs Touchett laughed. 'If it's dry, Isabel will water it. She is like a summer rain.'

'She is certainly very natural,' said Ralph. 'Where did you find this pretty cousin who I never knew about?'

Mrs Touchett told him. Then she asked, 'Do you think her so very pretty?'

'Very pretty,' said Ralph. 'And Warburton thinks she is interesting, too.'

His mother shook her head. 'Lord Warburton won't understand her. He needn't try.'

'He's very intelligent,' said Ralph. 'What does Isabel know about English lords?'

'Nothing,' said Mrs Touchett. 'But she will enjoy learning.'

Ralph laughed and looked out of the window. 'There's still time before dinner,' he said. 'Tell me some more. Won't Isabel give you trouble?'

'I hope not,' said Mrs Touchett. 'But the money question is a little difficult. She doesn't want my help, so she thinks she is going to pay her travel costs.'

'Ah, she's not rich,' said Ralph, 'but she likes to be independent. How interesting. Will you find her a husband?'

'Certainly not,' said Mrs Touchett. 'She is quite able to do that for herself.'

'Perhaps she has already chosen,' said Ralph.

'I don't know about a husband,' said Mrs Touchett, 'but there's a young man in Boston . . .'

'Come down to dinner now,' said Ralph. He didn't want to know about the young man in Boston.

Chapter 4   Getting to Know Lord Warburton

Isabel loved Gardencourt. Her uncle's old English house seemed like a picture from a book.

'It's a dear old place,' said Ralph, 'but I'm afraid it's very quiet for you. My father cannot leave his chair.'

The old man was very kind to Isabel. She often sat with him, asking questions about England and Queen Victoria. She wanted to know about the English people.

'Will I feel at home here?' she asked. 'Are they kind to young women?'

'I don't know about young women in the lower class, but I think women in the other classes are comfortable.'

'Goodness! How many classes are there?'

'I'm not sure,' said Mr Touchett. 'That's why it's good to be an American here. You don't belong to any class.'

Sometimes she took a boat on the river with Ralph, and sometimes they walked, but not far, because Ralph was not strong. He liked talking, but he was never serious.

One day, Isabel said angrily, 'You don't care for England, you don't care for America, what *do* you care for?'

'I care for nothing but you, dear cousin,' said Ralph, with a big smile.

Lord Warburton came to Gardencourt again, and stayed one night. 'Ralph is so lazy,' he said to Isabel. 'I am glad to see that he takes you boating.'

'Oh no,' laughed Ralph. 'I don't take Isabel – she takes *me*. My cousin does everything well, specially boating.'

Isabel asked Lord Warburton a great many questions too, and he answered them very carefully. Isabel was amused. 'He thinks I'm a wild thing, and that I've never seen forks and spoons,' she thought. In fact Lord Warburton knew more about the United States than Isabel. He was interesting and intelligent and kind.

When he left, Isabel said, 'I like your English lord very much.'

'So do I,' said Ralph. 'I love him. But I pity him more. He was born a lord, but he thinks this is wrong. He has modern ideas, but he can't change anything. You'll see, when we visit him at Lockleigh.'

The next week, Ralph and Mrs Touchett took her there. Lord Warburton showed Isabel his house, and she met his shy sisters. She realized that this great house belonged to a very old family, and Lord Warburton was its head.

Chapter 5   Henrietta Comes to Stay

When they returned to Gardencourt there was a letter waiting. Isabel showed it to her uncle. 'It's from my friend Henrietta,' she said. 'She writes for a newspaper in New York and they have sent her to London. She wants to see me.'

'Please ask her to visit us,' said Mr Touchett.

Isabel did so, but she wasn't sure it was a good idea. Henrietta Stackpole was the most independent woman that Isabel knew. She was not married, and had very little money, but she had a job, and she paid for her poor sister's children to go to school. Isabel admired her friend very much, but she didn't want her to write about Gardencourt and the Touchett family for her newspaper.

'So, she is a modern American woman,' said Ralph, while they were waiting at the station for Henrietta's train from London. 'Will I like her or will I dislike her?'

'It doesn't matter,' said Isabel. 'She doesn't care what men think of her.'

'Do you think she will write about us all for her newspaper?'

'I'll ask her not to,' Isabel answered.

'Then you think it's possible?'

'Perfectly.'

'Ah well, I think I will dislike her,' said Ralph.

'You'll probably fall in love with her at the end of three days.'

'And see my love letters in her newspaper? Never!'

But when Henrietta arrived, Ralph saw that she was a fresh, fair person with brave eyes and a high, clear voice, and he found it difficult not to like her at once.

Over the next few days, Ralph had many conversations with Henrietta. She spent the mornings writing in her room, and in the afternoons they walked together in the garden.

When Henrietta arrived, Ralph saw that she was a fresh,
fair person with brave eyes and a high clear voice.

'Do you people think of yourselves as American or English?' she asked him. 'I need to know how to talk to you.'

'Please talk to us anyway,' laughed Ralph.

'Do you always spend your time like this?'

'I don't usually spend it so pleasantly.'

'You know what I mean — you have no job.'

'Ah,' said Ralph, 'I'm the laziest man alive.'

'Why not go home to America?' said Henrietta. 'Find something to do — some new idea, some big work.'

'Isn't that very difficult?'

'Not if you put your heart into it.'

'Ah, my heart,' said Ralph.

'Haven't you got a heart?'

'I had one a few days ago, but I've lost it since.'

'Don't be funny,' said Henrietta.

◆

One morning, Henrietta showed her work to Isabel. 'Can I read this to you?' she said. 'I have written about Gardencourt.'

'I didn't want you to do that,' said Isabel.

Henrietta looked at her with clear eyes. 'Why, it's just what the people at home want, and it's a beautiful place.'

'It's too beautiful to go in the newspapers, and it's not what my uncle wants.'

'Then I won't do it,' said Henrietta, 'but it's a pity. Now Isabel, I have something to tell you. Caspar Goodwood is here too. We travelled on the same boat from America.'

'I know,' said Isabel. His letter was in her pocket. 'Dear Miss Archer,' it said, 'I have come to England. I cannot stay in America when you are not there. Can I see you again for half an hour? This is my dearest wish.'

Isabel could not decide how to answer this letter.

Chapter 6   Two Men with One Question

Lord Warburton soon visited Gardencourt again. It was a beautiful day, and he found Isabel in the garden. He wore a happy smile, and was ready to walk, or sit, or do anything that Isabel wanted to do.

He was also ready to do something which would surprise his friends. He knew a lot about Isabel's country, but very little about her family. She was not rich, and not the most beautiful woman that he knew. He counted no more than twenty-six hours with her since they met. But he cared nothing for these thoughts. He wanted to ask Isabel to marry him.

Isabel did not want to hear this question. She liked him, and she knew he would make a good husband. He was kind and honest. Why then did she hope he would not ask?

While she waited, Isabel touched the letter in her pocket. She liked Caspar very much too – a strong young man from her brave young country. England was not her country, and its rich old families had many rules. 'Can I ever be happy with an English lord?' she asked herself.

At last Lord Warburton asked his question.

'I thank you more than I can say, my lord,' said Isabel slowly, 'but I am not sure I want to marry anyone.'

'Oh, Miss Archer,' said Lord Warburton. 'Give me some hope. Please think it over for as long as you wish.'

'I will,' said Isabel, 'but please don't hope too much.'

After three days she wrote to him. 'You are very kind,' she said, 'but I cannot change my answer.'

She told her uncle, and he told her aunt. Mrs Touchett said, 'Do you hope to do something better?'

'I'm not sure of that,' said Isabel smiling. 'I just don't love Lord Warburton enough to marry him.'

'You did right to say no, then,' said Mrs Touchett.

◆

Soon it was time for Henrietta to return to London. She asked Isabel to go with her for a few days, and Ralph decided to go with them. Mr Touchett had a house in Winchester Square, but it was closed and cold, so they stayed in a hotel.

The three young people visited famous places in London – the British Museum more than once, the Tower of London, Westminster Abbey, and Kew Gardens.

On the third day, Isabel could see that Ralph was tired. 'Henrietta is busy with another friend tonight,' she said, 'so I will have a quiet dinner in my room.'

'Why can't I eat with you?' asked Ralph. 'Do you have another friend to see too?'

'No,' said Isabel. 'But you need to rest, and so do I.'

To her surprise, a visitor did come to see her in the hotel that evening. It was Caspar Goodwood.

'Why didn't you answer my letter?' he asked quickly.

'How did you know I was here?' replied Isabel, calmly.

'Henrietta told me. Can I stay?'

'You can sit down, certainly. Why are you here?'

'To follow you. I don't want to lose you.'

'You cannot lose what is not yours,' said Isabel.

'Why didn't you write to me,' he asked again.

Isabel said, 'I thought it was the best thing. I don't want you to think of me. Be strong.'

'I am strong,' said the young man, 'and that's why I love you more strongly.'

Isabel was silent. At last she said, 'Then think of me, but don't see me for a year or two. Don't follow me.'

'I'm not sure of that,' said Isabel smiling. 'I just don't
love Lord Warburton enough to marry him.'

'If I do that,' he replied, 'when will you marry me? That's the only question.'

'Probably never,' said Isabel. 'I really don't want to marry, or to talk about it. I must be independent.'

Chapter 7   Mysterious Madame Marle

When Ralph and Isabel returned to Gardencourt, Mr Touchett's health was worse. The days passed. Mrs Touchett did not speak of leaving for Paris.

There was another visitor in the house, a friend of Mrs Touchett's. When she first met Madame Merle, Isabel thought she was French, but she looked German with her thick fair hair and her large white hands.

'I'm American,' she told Isabel, 'but my husband was Swiss. Now I live in Rome.' In fact, Madame Merle had very little money, and liked to stay with rich friends like Mrs Touchett, who admired her greatly.

Isabel admired her too. Madame Merle talked well about books and pictures, and played the piano beautifully.

'I hope the music helps my uncle to feel better,' Isabel said to Ralph. 'Madame Merle plays so beautifully.'

'She does everything beautifully,' said Ralph.

Isabel looked at her cousin carefully. 'You don't like her,' she guessed.

Ralph's answer was strange. 'I loved her once,' he said, 'when her husband was alive.'

They did not speak about Madame Merle again. Ralph stayed with his father as much as he could. One day they spoke about money. 'I don't need a lot, Daddy,' said Ralph.

'Well, you'll have enough,' said Mr Touchett. 'Enough for two. The best thing that you can do, when I'm gone, is to marry.'

Madame Merle played the piano beautifully.

Ralph said nothing, and his father said softly. 'What do you think of your cousin?'

Ralph was silent for a long time. Then he said, 'I like Isabel very much, but I can't be in love with her because she's my cousin, and because I'm a sick man.'

'If you won't marry,' said Mr Touchett, 'what will you do when I'm not here to take care of? The bank does not interest you. What are your interests?'

Ralph answered his father carefully. 'I take a great interest in my cousin,' he said, 'but not the sort of interest that you want. I will not live for many years, but I hope I'll live long enough to see what Isabel does with her life. She is very inde-pendent. She does not need me. But I would like to do some-thing for her, Daddy. I would like her to be rich.'

'I'll do anything that you like,' said Mr Touchett, 'but I'm not sure it's right. Isabel's a sweet young thing, but if she is rich, will she be sensible?'

'She will do good things with the money,' said Ralph.

♦

Soon it was too cold to sit in the garden. Madame Merle spent her days writing letters, painting pictures, and playing the piano. To Isabel she seemed a wise woman of the world, but sometimes she said surprising things.

'I'd love to be your age again,' she said one day, 'to have my life before me again . . .'

'Your life is still before you,' said Isabel, sweetly.

'No. The best part has gone. I have no husband, no child, no fortune, and I am not beautiful now.'

'You have many friends, dear lady.'

'I am not so sure!' said Madame Merle.

♦

When she was not talking with her new friend, Isabel spent her time reading in the library. The house was very quiet. One afternoon she looked up to see Ralph in the doorway.

'It's finished,' he said. 'My dear father died an hour ago.'

'Ah, my poor Ralph!' said Isabel, putting out her two hands to him.

Chapter 8   Pansy and her Father

Six months later, on one of the first days of May, a small group of people sat in a beautiful room in a house on a hill above Florence. A young girl was looking at a picture.

A man watched her. 'Well, my dear, what do you think of it?' he asked, speaking in Italian.

'It's very pretty, Papa,' said the girl. 'Did you do paint it?'

'Certainly,' said the man. 'Don't you think I'm clever?'

Papa was forty, with a fine head and intelligent eyes. His thick hair was short and grey, and he wore a tidy beard.

The girl smiled at him sweetly. 'I, too, can paint pictures, Papa,' she said, and she looked across the room to where two nuns were sitting.

'She can paint very well,' said the older nun, in French, 'and she can play the piano.'

'Go into the garden,' said the father, also in French, 'and bring some flowers.' When the girl left, he said to the nuns, 'She's really very pretty. Is she good?'

'Oh yes, Monsieur,' said the younger nun. 'She's perfect. We love her too much. Pansy is like a daughter to us – she was so small when she came to us.'

'I do not want to take her away from you,' said the man.

'We're happy to hear that. Fifteen is very young.'

'I would like her to be with you always,' continued the man. 'But now, perhaps, I must have her with me.'

'Ah Monsieur,' said the older nun, smiling and standing up. 'She is good, but she is for the world, not for us.'

Pansy returned with two bunches of roses, one white and the other red. She gave them to the nuns with a kiss. They were saying goodbye when a new visitor came into the room.

The man looked surprised, but stood still and said nothing. The young girl gave a soft little cry: 'Ah, Madame Merle!'

'Yes, it's Madame Merle. I've come to welcome you home,' said the visitor, and she held out two hands to the girl.

'These ladies have brought my daughter home and now they are returning to Rome,' the man explained.

'I have just come from Rome,' said Madame Merle. 'It's very beautiful there now.'

'She came to see me at school,' Pansy told her father.

'Madame Merle is a good friend to us,' he explained to the nuns. 'She will help us to decide if my daughter can return to you in Rome at the end of the holidays.'

'I decide nothing,' laughed Madame Merle. 'I know your school is good, but it is expensive, and Mr Osmond must of course remember that Miss Osmond is for the world.'

'That's what I told monsieur,' said the older nun.

'Am I not for you, Papa?' asked Pansy in her clear, soft voice.

Osmond laughed. 'For me and for the world, Pansy.'

The nuns left, Pansy returned to the garden, and Madame Merle now spoke to Osmond in English.

'I've been in Florence for a week – at Palazzo Crescentini with Mrs Touchett. I hoped you would visit me.'

'I didn't know you were there.'

'It's not important to me, but perhaps it will be important to you. When did you last make a new friend?'

'You were the last. I don't want new friends.'

*Pansy returned with two bunches of roses, one white
and the other red.*

'You're too lazy, Gilbert. It is time for you to meet another. Her name is Isabel Archer. She's American. Mrs Touchett is her aunt.'

'And why must I meet Miss Archer? Is she beautiful, clever, rich and good?'

'She's young – twenty-three years old. I like her a lot. Yes, she is beautiful and intelligent, and, for an American, she comes from a good family.'

'And is she rich?'

'Mr Touchett left her seventy thousand pounds.'

Chapter 9   Isabel Meets Gilbert Osmond

When Mr Touchett died, Mrs Touchett sold his London house. Ralph kept Gardencourt but he soon left England to spend the winter in Italy.

Mrs Touchett was surprised to learn about Isabel's fortune. She told her friend Madame Merle.

'Ah, the clever girl,' said Madame Merle.

Mrs Touchett gave her a quick look. 'What do you mean?'

Madame Merle dropped her eyes. 'I mean it's clever to get a fortune without trying,' she said.

'She certainly didn't try,' said Mrs Touchett. 'It was Ralph's idea. She never knew of it.'

And that was true. At first Isabel couldn't understand how rich she was. 'Is it good for me?' she asked her aunt.

'It can't be bad for you,' said Mrs Touchett. 'Of course you don't have to stay with your boring old aunt now. Perhaps you can ask Miss Stackpole to travel with you.'

'I don't think you're boring,' Isabel replied to this, and they agreed to travel together to Paris and Italy.

Henrietta was not ready to leave England, but she planned

to visit Europe soon, with some friends. She knew that Caspar Goodwood was now back in America. 'I hope you gave him some hope for the future,' she said to Isabel.

'I asked Mr Goodwood not to speak about marriage,' said Isabel, 'and I must ask you the same, Henrietta.'

'Isabel Archer,' said her friend, seriously, 'if you marry one of these people I'll never speak to you again.'

Isabel thought of Lord Warburton, and smiled to herself. She had said no to 'one of these people', but she certainly didn't want Henrietta to know that.

The two friends said goodbye, and agreed to meet again in Italy.

◆

Isabel and her aunt visited Paris, and then joined Ralph in Florence. There, in Mrs Touchett's old and beautiful house, Isabel also met Madame Merle again, and when Gilbert Osmond came to visit Madame Merle, Isabel met him too. He asked her to visit his house on the hill, to meet his daughter and to take tea in the garden.

Isabel enjoyed the visit. While Madame Merle sat in the garden with Pansy, Osmond showed Isabel all his beautiful things. 'I, too, am American,' he explained, 'but I like the old world. I like fine old things. I'm not rich, so I cannot buy much, but what I buy is always perfect.'

After that visit, Gilbert Osmond came often to Palazzo Crescentini. 'Do you think he wants to marry Isabel?' asked Mrs Touchett. 'He has only a few fine pictures and a pretty daughter.'

'Isabel likes the poor child,' said Madame Merle.

'The child can't hope to marry without a fortune,' said Mrs Touchett. 'Isabel is kind – I hope she is careful too.'

Isabel was happy in Florence, but sometimes her thoughts

went back to two men, Caspar Goodwood and Lord Warburton. She hoped they were not unhappy, and pictured them with better wives than she could ever be. She did not realize that she would see one of them again soon.

Chapter 10 Choosing a Husband

In the same way that he once wanted Isabel to see London, now Ralph wanted her to see Rome. They decided to go there to meet Henrietta and her friends.

'You'll like Rome,' said Gilbert Osmond when Isabel told him her plans. 'I'd like to see you there.'

'Then why don't you come with us?' said Isabel.

'Perhaps I will,' said Osmond. 'Perhaps I'll join you there. First I must ask someone to take care of Pansy.'

After Isabel and Ralph left Florence, Osmond told Madame Merle about this conversation.

'She wants me to go to Rome with her,' he said in a low voice.

'I'm glad to hear it. Of course you'll go.'

'Ah,' said Osmond. 'You want me to work hard for this plan of yours.'

'I'm sure you enjoy it,' said Madame Merle with a smile.

'I do like her,' said Osmond.

'Good.'

'But there's just one problem. She has too many ideas.'

'Ah yes, she is clever.'

'The ideas must stop,' said Osmond.

Madame Merle looked at him and said nothing. Then he said, 'If I go to Rome what will I do with Pansy?'

'I'll go and see her,' said Madame Merle.

♦

'You'll like Rome,' said Gilbert Osmond when Isabel told
him her plans. 'I'd like to see you there.'

Lord Warburton was in Rome. He found Isabel one afternoon while she was resting on a stone in the Forum. The sky was blue and clear, and when she looked up she saw him.

'Lord Warburton!' she said, standing up.

'I didn't know you were here,' he said. 'I was travelling in the East – Turkey and Greece. Now I'm returning to England. Can I sit down?'

'I'm with my cousin,' said Isabel. 'He's over there with some friends. Please wait for him.'

It was difficult to talk. Lord Warburton was clearly unhappy. When Ralph and Henrietta came, it was easier. The two men were very pleased to be together again. Lord Warburton met the other people in their little group, and then he walked away with Ralph.

'Who is the older man?' Lord Warburton asked Ralph.

'His name's Gilbert Osmond – he lives in Florence.'

'Does Isabel like him?'

'She's not sure yet.'

'Is he very clever?'

'Very,' said Ralph, and took his friend by the arm.

That evening they all went to the theatre. In the dark, Lord Warburton watched Isabel. He left early.

'Poor Lord Warburton,' said Isabel. 'He's a nice man.'

'He's very lucky,' said Osmond. 'A great lord, handsome, and Isabel likes him. Why do you call him poor?'

Ralph said, 'Women, after they hurt a man, often pity him. They think it is kind to do that.'

Osmond realized that the English lord loved Isabel.

Two days later, Lord Warburton met Isabel again. 'I'm leaving Rome,' he said, 'so I must say goodbye.'

Isabel was sorry to hear it, but she didn't say so.

'You don't care what I do,' said Lord Warburton, sadly. 'When will I see you again?'

Isabel was quiet, then she said, 'After you're married.'

'That will never be,' said Lord Warburton. 'It will be after you are married.' And they said goodbye.

Then Isabel had a letter from Mrs Touchett. 'Will you come back to Florence?' she asked. 'It is time to travel again. Do you want to come with me?'

Isabel replied quickly to say 'yes', and Ralph agreed to take her back to Florence the next day. That evening, in the rose-coloured sitting-room of their hotel, Isabel told Osmond about her plans to travel. She was going away for many months.

'Go everywhere, do everything, be happy,' said Osmond. 'But you'll be tired some day. Shall I wait until then to say what I want to say?'

'I don't know until you say it,' said Isabel, lightly.

He looked at the ground. 'I find I'm in love with you.'

'Ah,' said Isabel quickly. 'Keep that until I *am* tired.'

'No, hear it now,' said Osmond, looking up. 'I have little to give you. I have no fortune, and I'm not famous. But for me you're the most important woman in the world.'

'Please go now,' said Isabel. 'Goodnight.'

♦

One year later Isabel returned to Florence. In the late spring, she agreed to marry Gilbert Osmond.

Chapter 11   Caspar's Visit

Isabel told Caspar Goodwood first. She wrote to him in Boston, and he left immediately for Florence. By ship and train his journey took seventeen days. Caspar arrived late one night and went straight to see Isabel in the morning.

*Caspar arrived late one night and went straight to see
Isabel in the morning.*

'Are you very tired?' asked Isabel.

'I'm never tired,' said Caspar Goodwood. 'Now tell me, who and what is Mr Gilbert Osmond?'

'Who and what? Nobody and nothing but a good and quiet man. He's not in business, and he isn't rich or famous.'

'In your letter you say he's American. Doesn't he like the United States?'

'He never goes there. He's happy in Italy.'

'I thought you didn't want to marry.'

'No one can be more surprised than me,' she said slowly.

'You told me to wait two years.'

'I promised nothing. I was perfectly free.'

He was silent for quite some time. To change the subject, Isabel asked, 'Have you seen Henrietta Stackpole?'

'Yes,' said Goodwood. 'She's busy with her writing work in America, but I think she wants to see more of Europe. Does she know Mr Osmond?'

'A little,' said Isabel. 'And she doesn't like him. But of course I'm not marrying to please Henrietta.'

He was silent again for some time. 'Well,' he said at last. 'I've seen you, which is what I wanted. I will not trouble you again.' He went to the door, without shaking hands. At the door he stopped and said, 'I'll leave Florence tomorrow.' He was very calm, but she was not.

'I am glad to hear it,' she said. For some minutes after he left she did feel glad, then suddenly she began to cry.

◆

The next day, Isabel told her aunt. 'There is nothing *of* Osmond,' said Mrs Touchett, 'no money, no name, no importance. Don't you care for these things?'

Isabel said, 'I care very much for money, and that's why I want Mr Osmond to have some.'

27

'Give it to him then,' said her aunt, 'but don't marry him.'

Mrs Touchett told Ralph. He said nothing about it for three days. He was looking very sick, and sat quietly in the garden while Isabel went out walking with her lover. At last he said, 'I had great hopes for you, Isabel.'

Isabel didn't understand, and Ralph couldn't explain. He wanted Isabel's money to make her free. Now Isabel wanted to use the money to help Osmond. Isabel was warm and honest but Ralph thought Osmond was cold and small. He chose only perfect things and Isabel was just another perfect thing.

It was clear to Isabel that they did not like Gilbert Osmond, but she did not worry. She was not marrying him to please the Touchetts.

Pansy, now sixteen and a little taller, was more polite. 'You will be good for papa,' she said. 'You're both so quiet and so serious.'

'I'll be very kind to you, my good little Pansy,' said Isabel.

And she was.

Soon after the marriage the family moved to a big house in Rome. A year later a baby was born, but the poor little boy died after six months. Isabel quietly watched Pansy grow up.

Chapter 12   Osmond's Plan for Pansy

When Pansy was nineteen she fell in love. She said nothing about it to her father, but Isabel knew. The young man was Ned Rosier, an American who lived in Paris. When he travelled to Rome, he always visited Isabel's 'evenings'.

'Mrs Osmond,' he said to Isabel, watching Pansy serve tea. 'You must help me. I want to marry Pansy. I have enough money.'

Isabel held her 'evenings' on Thursdays. Osmond asked only

the best people, but Isabel welcomed her old friends. Ned Rosier was the son of her father's friend.

'Your fortune is enough for Pansy, Mr Rosier,' she said, 'but I'm afraid it isn't large enough for her father.'

Isabel now knew that her marriage was not happy. Osmond thought she had too many ideas. He told her that one day. Too many ideas? Didn't married people like to talk about ideas? She began to understand that the only ideas Osmond wanted her to have were his ideas. He wanted to change her. He didn't want her to be strong and independent – he wanted her just to be pretty, like Pansy. But Isabel could not change. She realized that when she fell in love with Osmond she saw only half the man. Now she began to see all of him.

She said nothing to Ralph, though she knew he was right about Osmond. Ralph was staying in a hotel near her house. Osmond didn't like Isabel visiting Ralph in the hotel, but Ralph was very sick. Isabel was afraid he was dying.

'You really mustn't travel,' she said. 'Why did Lord Warburton agree to bring you here?'

'He knows I live only for you,' laughed Ralph, weakly.

Ralph was too sick to leave the hotel, but Lord Warburton came to the Osmonds' house every Thursday evening. He talked a lot to Pansy. Osmond was watching.

'Perhaps Lord Warburton wishes to marry Pansy,' he said.

Madame Merle said the same.

After her marriage, Isabel did not see much of Madame Merle. She was often away, but now she was in Rome again, and she was careful not to see the Osmonds too often.

'I am careful,' she told Isabel, 'because I don't want you to worry. Sometimes a husband's old friend can forget that his wife will worry if she thinks they are together too much.'

Isabel did not worry in this way, but one day she came into a room and saw them together. Madame Merle was standing, and Osmond was sitting. 'How strange,' thought Isabel. 'I know they're old friends, but Osmond is always very polite.'

'Ah, Isabel,' said Madame Merle, when she saw her. 'We're speaking of Pansy. Does Lord Warburton love her?'

'I don't know,' said Isabel, 'but Pansy does not love him.'

'Pansy will do as I say,' said Osmond. 'Lord Warburton loved you, Isabel, so I know you can help. Please do what you can. It will be a great marriage.'

Isabel thought about it and decided that she agreed. 'Pansy will be perfect at Lockleigh,' she said to herself, 'if Lord Warburton can be happy with her.' She wanted to be sure, so she asked her cousin, 'Is Lord Warburton in love?'

'Very much, I think,' said Ralph, 'but not with Pansy. If he wants to marry her, it's because he wants to be near you.'

Isabel was silent. Ralph watched her. He knew she was unhappy, and he knew she didn't like to speak of it. 'Ah, my dear Isabel,' he said at last. 'I wanted so much for you.'

She kissed him. 'You're my best friend,' she said.

Chapter 13   Madame Merle's Secret

One evening, Isabel took Pansy to a great party. Osmond stayed at home because he didn't like to dance. Pansy loved dancing, and Lord Warburton and Isabel sat watching her.

'I'm forty-two years old, Mrs Osmond,' he said. 'Will Pansy marry me?'

'She will wish to please her father,' said Isabel.

'Then I will send him my letter,' said Warburton. 'I wrote it today, but I wanted to speak to you first.'

Isabel smiled at Ned Rosier, who was standing near them. Lord Warburton followed her smile. 'Why does that man look so sad?' he asked.

'Ah, my dear Isabel,' he said at last. 'I wanted
so much for you.'

'Because he isn't rich and he isn't clever. But he cares for Pansy, and Pansy cares for him.'

Isabel saw the surprise on Lord Warburton's face, and changed the subject.

Three days later he came to tell the Osmonds that he was returning to England. Ralph was very sick, to sick to travel, but Lord Warburton knew that he wanted too die at Gardencourt. He said nothing of marriage to Pansy, and nothing to give Osmond hope for the future.

Osmond did not like Ralph, and was pleased he was leaving Rome. To Lord Warburton he was coldly polite. He called Pansy to say goodbye.

'I'm going away,' said Lord Warburton. 'And I want to tell you how much I hope you will be very happy.'

'Thank you, Lord Warburton,' said Pansy softly.

Looking at Isabel he said, 'I'm sure you will be happy – you've got a very good friend.' Pansy smiled sweetly and said goodbye.

He shook hands with Isabel silently, and soon he left.

Isabel knew Osmond was very angry, and waited for him to speak of it. He said to her at last, 'You've played a very deep game.'

'I've no idea what you mean,' Isabel replied.

'I thought Warburton wrote me a letter – that's what you told me.'

'That's what he told me.'

'Where is it then?'

'I've no idea. I didn't ask him.'

'I'm sure you stopped the letter,' said Osmond. 'I can't forgive you. Everyone will laugh at me now, because I tried to marry my daughter to a lord.' Isabel saw that he cared nothing for his daughter's happiness.

Osmond sent Pansy back to the nuns for a time. 'I want my

daughter to be fresh and soft,' he explained. 'Pansy's life is getting a little too fast – she needs to rest. I like to think of her in that old place. She will have her books, she can paint, and she will have her piano. I want her to have time to think.'

He never spoke about Warburton again, but Madame Merle did. 'What did you do to send Lord Warburton away?' she asked Isabel angrily. 'That was not kind to Pansy.'

'Pansy doesn't care for him. She's very glad he's gone,' said Isabel.

'I know he once asked you to marry him. Did you want to keep his love?' said Madame Merle. 'I wanted this marriage so much. Why did you stop us from having him?'

These words surprised Isabel. 'Who are you – what are you?' she asked in a quiet voice. 'What are you to my husband?'

'Everything,' replied Madame Merle. 'I made your marriage, and I wanted to make Pansy's too.'

'Why?' asked Isabel. 'What are you to us?'

'I am Pansy's mother,' said Madame Merle.

Chapter 14   'My Cousin Is Dying'

Isabel could not stop thinking about Madame Merle's words and her ugly secret. She realized that she knew nothing of the first Mrs Osmond – did she die before Pansy was born? When did Madame Merle's husband die? Why didn't Osmond marry her? She thought about how much Osmond loved money. Did Madame Merle choose Isabel for Osmond because of her fortune?

Mrs Touchett wrote to Isabel from Gardencourt: 'Ralph is near the end. He wants to see you if you are not too busy.' Isabel went immediately to her husband.

'I must go to Gardencourt,' she told him. 'My cousin is dying.'

'Your cousin was dying when we married,' said Osmond. 'He will continue to live.'

'I want to see him before he dies,' said Isabel.

'But I don't want you to go,' said her husband.

Isabel realized she must choose the right thing to do. She loved Ralph and she must see him, but Osmond was very angry. 'The world thinks we have a perfect marriage,' he said. 'If you go against my wishes, everyone will know it's not true. A marriage, Isabel, is a very important thing.'

Isabel agreed with this, but she said, 'I can see you're afraid I will not come back,' and she left the same night.

On her way to the train she visited the nuns, to see Pansy. 'I've come to say goodbye,' she said. 'I'm going to England.'

Pansy's white little face turned red. 'To England! When will you come back?'

'I don't know, Pansy. My cousin is very sick. I wish to see him.'

'Ah yes, of course you must go. And will papa go?'

'No,' said Isabel.

The girl said nothing for a time, then she looked at Isabel and said, 'You're not happy, Mrs Osmond. Perhaps you won't come back?'

'Perhaps not. I can't tell.'

'Don't leave me here,' said Pansy softly.

Isabel's heart went faster. 'Will you come away with me now?'

'Did papa say that?'

'No, it's my idea.'

'Then I must wait here,' said Pansy, sadly. 'But when you're not here I am a little afraid.'

'What are you afraid of?'

'Don't leave me here,' said Pansy softly.

'Of papa – a little. And of Madame Merle. She was here tonight. I don't like her.'

'You must never say that,' said Isabel.

They walked together to the top of the stairs. 'Goodbye, my child,' said Isabel, as she started to go down.

'You'll come back?' called Pansy, in a voice that Isabel could never forget.

'Yes – I'll come back.'

Madame Merle was waiting for Isabel downstairs. 'I know Pansy does not like me,' she explained, 'but I came to say goodbye.'

Isabel said nothing.

'You're very unhappy, I know,' said Madame Merle. 'But I am more so. I am going to live in America. And you? To England? Ah, poor Ralph! Did you know it was his idea to give you a fortune?'

Chapter 15   Saying Goodbye

On the long train journey Isabel felt dead. At Gardencourt, waiting for her aunt to welcome her, she thought of that wet afternoon in America when they first met. 'Caspar Goodwood came to see me the same day,' she remembered. 'Was I right not to marry him?'

Isabel sat next to Ralph's bed, without hope. He knew her, but could not speak for three days. At last he said, 'Ah, Isabel, with me it's finished. I am glad you came. And what about you?'

Suddenly Isabel put her head in her hands and started to cry. Ralph lay silent, listening to her.

'What have you done for me, Ralph?' she cried. 'I never knew. I never thanked you. Is it true – is it true?'

'Your fortune?' he said. 'Yes, it's true. It was my idea, but it was a mistake.'

'Osmond married me for the money,' said Isabel. She wanted to speak honestly now.

'And now you are unhappy. Will you go back to him?'

'I don't know – I can't tell. I just want to stay here.'

'Please stay here,' said Ralph. 'Be happy. And keep me in your heart. Remember that I've always loved you.'

'Oh, my brother,' she cried.

The next morning Ralph was dead.

◆

Three days later, many important people came to the church near Gardencourt. Isabel knew only Lord Warburton and one tall American. Why was he there? They did not speak.

Isabel stayed at Gardencourt, with no thoughts for the future. Her aunt was busy. Lord Warburton came to tell them he planned to marry an English girl, and Isabel was glad.

One evening, while she was sitting in the garden, she saw a tall shadow. 'Don't be afraid,' said Caspar Goodwood, quickly. 'I came from London by train today. I want to help you. I visited your cousin before he died. He told me about you – I know you are unhappy. He asked me to look after you. And I can, Isabel. The world is very big. We'll never be afraid together. Be mine, as I am yours.'

Isabel had a sudden feeling of danger. 'Please go away,' she said. She was crying now.

'Ah, don't say that. Don't kill me!' said Caspar, and he kissed her hard. To Isabel the kiss was white-hot. It seemed to be something to rest on. Slowly she moved from darkness to light. Slowly she knew where to go. There was a very straight road.

When Caspar Goodwood came to Gardencourt again two days later, they told him. 'Mrs Osmond has gone to London.

'Ah, don't say that. Don't kill me!' said Caspar.

She is with Miss Stackpole.' He knew Henrietta was back in Europe again, and he went straight to the house where she was staying. Henrietta answered the door.

'Oh, good morning,' he said. 'I was hoping to find Mrs Osmond.'

Henrietta looked at him. 'She was here yesterday, and spent the night,' she said. 'But this morning she started for Rome.'

Caspar Goodwood could not move.

Henrietta touched his arm. 'Mr Goodwood,' she said kindly, 'just you wait.' But he thought she was wrong to give him hope.

ACTIVITIES

Chapters 1–5

Before you read

1 What kind of story do you think this will be? A story about love? or crime? or adventure? Say why. The pictures in the book will help you.

2 All these words come in this part of the story. Find their meanings in your dictionary. Then put them in the correct places in the sentences below.

admire   care for   certainly   class   independent   thoughts   wish

After they met, his ..... soon turned to marriage, because he ..... her very much. He belonged to a higher ..... than she did but she knew that he ..... her. She ..... didn't want to get married immediately: her real ..... was to be ..... for a time.

3 One of the people in the story is a *lord*. This means that he is:

   a a soldier and high officer

   b a man with a title

   c a man who owns a lot of land

After you read

4 Change these sentences to make them true.

   a After her father died, Isabel had a lot of money.

   b She decided to leave America with her sisters.

   c First she went to her uncle's house in Italy.

   d She made friends with her English cousin Ralph.

5 In Chapter 5, Ralph says: 'I think I will dislike her.'

   a Who is he talking about?

   b What did he think of her when they met?

6 Answer these questions:

   a Who writes to Isabel?

   b What does he ask for in the letter?

40

Chapters 6–10

Before you read

7 What does *fortune* mean:
   a bad weather
   b a large amount of money
   c a kind of cake

8 In Chapter 9, Henrietta speaks of 'hope for the future'. What word means the opposite of *future*?

9 On which page can you find a picture of two *nuns*?

10 Do you think that Isabel will stay in Europe or return to the United States? Why? Talk about this with other students.

After you read

11 Answer these questions:
   a At Gardencourt, what does Lord Warburton ask Isabel?
   b How does Isabel reply?
   c Caspar says: 'I don't want to lose you.' What answer does Isabel give?

12 In Chapter 7, Isabel says: 'My poor Ralph!' Why?

13 In Florence:
   a Where did Isabel stay?
   b Who helped Gilbert Osmond to meet her?
   c What did Osmond know about Isabel?

14 In Rome:
   a Who was Isabel surprised to meet again?
   b What did Osmond ask Isabel?

Chapters 11–15

Before you read

15 Do you think that the story will end happily or unhappily for Isabel? Say why.

16 Who says these things and what do they mean?

    a 'I will not trouble you again.'

    b 'Your fortune is enough for Pansy but I'm afraid it isn't large enough for her father.'

    c 'I'm sure you will be happy – you've got a very good friend.'

17 Four men love Isabel in different ways: Caspar Goodwood, Lord Warburton, Ralph Touchett and Gilbert Osmond. Talk about these men. In what ways is their love for Isabel different? Why was Osmond the wrong one to marry?

18 At the end of the story Isabel leaves for Rome because of a promise she made.

    a Who did she make the promise to?

    b What was the promise?

Writing

19 Describe a day which Isabel spends with her friends visiting famous places in London or in Rome.

20 You are Madame Merle. Write a letter to Pansy in which you tell her that you are her real mother.

21 Write a different ending to the story in which both Isabel and Pansy are truly happy.

22 Write a note about this book to a friend. Say if you think they will like it or dislike it and give your reasons.

Answers for the Activities in this book are published in our free resource packs for teachers, the Penguin Readers Factsheets, or available on a separate sheet. Please write to your local Pearson Education office or to: Marketing Department, Penguin Longman Publishing, 5 Bentinck Street, London W1M 5RN.